Minerals

Connor Dayton

PowerKiDS press™

New York

Published in 2007 by The Rosen Publishing Group, Inc.
29 East 21st Street, New York, NY 10010

First Edition

Editor: Jennifer Way
Book Design: Greg Tucker

Photo Credits: Cover, pp. 5, 7, 11, 13, 15, 17, 19, 19 (inset) Shutterstock.com; p. 5 (inset) © Breck P. Kent/Animals Animals/Earth Scenes; p. 9 © Paul Silverman/Fundamental Photographs; p. 21 © Salvatore Vasapolli/Animals Animals/Earth Scenes.

Library of Congress Cataloging-in-Publication Data

Dayton, Connor.
   Minerals / Connor Dayton. — 1st ed.
      p. cm. — (Rocks and minerals)
   Includes index.
   ISBN-13: 978-1-4042-3691-2 (library binding)
   ISBN-10: 1-4042-3691-0 (library binding)
   1. Minerals—Juvenile literature. I. Title. II. Series.

QE365.2.D39 2007
549—dc22

                                    2006031126

Manufactured in the United States of America

Contents

What Are Minerals?

Minerals are **inorganic compounds** that can be found in nature. They are **solids** that have a crystal structure. Crystal structure means the way in which the smallest parts of the mineral are held together. Minerals may be made up of one **element** or of many elements. Minerals make up the rocks that you see around you every day.

This book will show you a few of the most common types of minerals. It will explain how minerals are put together and how what they are made of makes them special.

There are around 4,000 known minerals. This shiny dark gray mineral is mica. *Inset:* This is a mineral called feldspar.

Crystals and Chemistry

Chemistry and crystal structure are two main ways in which minerals are classified, or grouped. A mineral's chemistry means the mix of different elements that make up that mineral. Its crystal structure is the way that the tiniest parts of each mineral, its atoms, are put together.

Two or more minerals can have the same crystal structure but be made up of different chemicals. Two or more minerals also can have the same chemical makeup but have different crystal structures. These are called polymorphs. Crystal structure and chemistry work together to decide a mineral's **properties**.

This is a mineral called fluorite. One of fluorite's properties is that it glows a different color under special lights. This property is called fluorescence.

Properties of Minerals

A mineral's properties make it look and **react** differently from other minerals. Properties can be used to identify, or name, minerals.

Many minerals are known for having a special color. Minerals also have luster, which is how shiny or dull the mineral looks. Minerals also can have a streak. This is the color that appears when a mineral is rubbed against something. It is sometimes different from the mineral's color.

Minerals can be classified in other ways, such as their **specific gravity**, **magnetism**, how they break, or their hardness. The Mohs' scale is used to **compare** the hardnesses of minerals.

4 Fluorite

5 Apatite

6 Orthoclase

7 Quartz

3 Calcite

2 Gypsum

1 Talc

10 Diamond

8 Topaz

9 Corundum

The Mohs' scale uses 10 minerals to help people compare mineral hardness. Talc is the softest and can be cut by the other minerals. Diamond is the hardest and cannot be cut by any other mineral.

Elements

Elements make up all the matter on Earth. There are 116 different elements in the world. Most minerals are compounds of two or more elements. However, some minerals have a very simple chemistry. They are made up of only one kind of element. This means that these minerals are also elements.

Examples of elements that are also minerals are bismuth, sulphur, and graphite. There are also many **metals** that are both minerals and elements. These are called **precious** metals.

Sulphur is a mineral that is also an element. Two of its properties are that it is yellow and that it smells like rotten eggs.

Precious Metals

Some minerals are called precious metals. These are minerals that are made up of one metallic element. They are called precious because they are uncommon and have a high value for many people. Because of their value, some precious metals, such as gold and silver, have been used as money.

Precious metals have a few properties in common. They do not often mix with other elements to form compounds. Many have a shiny luster and need a lot of heat before they will melt.

Gold is one of the highly valued precious metals. It is generally valued at around 50 times the cost of the same amount of silver.

Oxides and Sulfides

Oxides and sulfides are two large groupings of minerals. They make up many of the compounds you see every day. Oxides are compounds that have the element oxygen in them. They make compounds with many useful metals, such as iron, that are mined, or dug from the ground.

Sulfides are compounds that have the element sulphur in them. They also make compounds with metals and can be mined. Pyrite is the name for iron sulfide. It is also known as fool's gold because it looks a lot like gold.

This is iron sulfide, or fool's gold. It can be hard to tell pyrite from gold by looks alone.

Silicates

Silicates are the largest group of minerals. They are made of the elements silicon and oxygen, which then form compounds with other elements. Aluminum, iron, and calcium are a few examples of common minerals that form silicate compounds.

Because they are so common, silicates make up at least a part of most of Earth's rocks. That means that almost every rock you pick up likely has silicates in it. Silicates can be found in quartz, as well as in many gemstones.

Quartz is one of the most common silicates on Earth. It can be many colors. This piece of quartz is purple, pink, and red.

Carbonates and Sulfates

Carbonates and sulfates are mineral groupings that have some things in common. Carbonates are compounds that have the element carbon in them. They most often form compounds with minerals such as calcium.

Sulfates are another kind of compound that has the element sulphur in it. They most often form compounds with the same kinds of elements with which carbonates form compounds. Both carbonates and sulfates tend to form in places where salt water evaporates, or dries up.

Calcium carbonate, or calcite, can build up into formations inside caves called stalactites and stalagmites. *Inset:* Gypsum is a sulfate that is made up of water and the minerals calcium and sulphur.

Halides

Halide minerals are often thought of as different kinds of salts. Halides are compounds that have the elements flourine, chlorine, or iodine in them. The salt in your kitchen is a compound of the elements sodium and chlorine.

As are the sulfates, halides often form where salt water evaporates. You can see halides in places such as the Bonneville Salt Flats, in Utah. This is a very flat place where the salt minerals have formed and totally covered the ground.

This salt flat is in Death Valley's Badwater Basin, in California. This is a very hot and dry place. When rain does fall, it carries salt minerals from the mountain rocks to the basin. Evaporation then leads to a buildup of salt in the basin.

Minerals and the Formation of Rocks

Minerals make up the rocks that you see every day and all the different kinds of rocks that make up Earth. Some minerals are found deep under ground. People mine to get to these minerals. Some are valued for their usefulness, and others are valued for their beauty.

Minerals are in the stones that are used to build houses. They are in the gold and silver **jewelry** you wear and in the soda cans from which you drink. You can find minerals almost everywhere you look!

Glossary

chemistry (KEH-mih-stree) The makeup of matter.

compare (kum-PER) To see how two or more things are alike or unlike.

compounds (KOM-powndz) Two or more things put together.

element (EH-luh-ment) The basic matter of which all things are made.

inorganic (in-or-GA-nik) Not living.

jewelry (JOO-ul-ree) Objects worn on the body that are made of special metals, such as gold and silver, and valued stones.

magnetism (MAG-nuh-tih-zum) The force that pulls certain objects toward each other.

metals (MEH-tulz) Hard matter that is shiny, hard, and can easily be shaped.

precious (PREH-shus) Having a high value or price.

properties (PRAH-pur-teez) Things that describe something.

react (ree-AKT) To act because something has happened.

solids (SO-ledz) Hard matter.

specific gravity (spih-SIH-fik GRA-vuh-tee) The heaviness of a mineral.

Index

C
crystal structure, 4, 6

E
Earth, 10, 14, 22
element(s), 4, 6, 10, 12, 16, 18

G
gold, 12, 14

H
hardness(es), 8

I
iron, 14

L
luster, 8, 12

M
magnetism, 8

metals, 10, 12, 14
Mohs' scale, 8

P
polymorphs, 6
pyrite, 14

S
specific gravity, 8
streak, 8

Web Sites

Due to the changing nature of Internet links, PowerKids Press has developed an online list of Web sites related to the subject of this book. This site is updated regularly. Please use this link to access the list:
www.powerkidslinks.com/romi/min/